The World of the Unknown
ALL ABOUT GHOSTS

An American Indian legend tells of the flying head of a phantom warrior which had the wings of a bat and the claws of an eagle.

Phantom coaches often feature in ghost stories. Drivers and horses are almost always headless. The one shown here, spotted in the 1800's is an exception to the rule.

The most famous phantom ship is the Flying Dutchman, doomed to sail the seas forever. Sailors often claimed to have seen this ship when making the perilous journey around the Cape of Good Hope off South Africa. Sighting the Dutchman was supposed to be an omen of disaster.

Credits

Written by
Christopher Maynard
Art and editorial direction
David Jefferis
Text editing by
Ingrid Selberg
Designed by
John Jamieson
Design assistant
Iain Ashman
Picture research
Caroline Lucas
Special consultant
Eric Maple
Illustrators
Roland Berry
Gordon Davies
John Francis
Brian Lewis
Malcolm McGregor
Michael Roffe
Special photography
John Jamieson
Christopher Maynard

Acknowledgements
We wish to thank the following
individuals and organizations for
their assistance and for making
available information and
photographs from their
collections.
Harry Price library
RF Lord
Mary Evans Picture Library
National Laboratory of
Psychical Research
Psychic News
Radio Times Hulton
Picture Library
SPR (Society for Psychical
Research)
Syndication International

Printed in Belgium by
Henri Proost, Turnhout,
Belgium.

First published in 1977 by
Usborne Publishing Ltd
20 Garrick Street
London WC2E 9BJ

© 1977 Usborne
Publishing Ltd

The World of the Unknown

ALL ABOUT

GHOSTS

About this book

Contents

This book is for anyone who has shivered at shadowy figures in the dark, heard strange sounds in the night or felt the presence of a mysterious 'something' from the unknown.

Ghost stories are as old as recorded history and exist all over the world. Many of the different kinds of ghosts that are thought to haunt the Earth and their behaviour are described here. You will meet haunting spirits, screaming skulls, phantom ships, demon dogs, white ladies, gallows ghosts and many more.

This book also explains the techniques and equipment of ghost hunting and tells how lots of 'ghosts' have been exposed as fakes or explained away as natural events. Also included are some of the recent theories which attempt to explain the possible existence of ghosts.

What is a ghost?

Ghosts are supposed to be the appearances of the spirits of the dead in a form visible to the living.

According to those who have claimed to see ghosts, they usually look pale and cloudy. They can pass through solid objects such as doors and walls. They appear and vanish leaving no trace.

Whether they really do exist is still a complete mystery, but perhaps this book will help you to make up your mind.

The story told below has many features associated with the creation of a ghost.

Tom Colley's ghost

In 1751, near the town of Tring in England, an old couple were beaten and drowned by a frenzied mob who thought they were witches. The leader of the mob, Tom Colley, was later arrested and sentenced to death by hanging. When he was dead, his body was suspended from the gallows (like that shown on the right) inside a gibbet – a cage of iron hoops and chains. It was left to dangle there as a gruesome warning to other lawbreakers.

People believed that a person's spirit could not leave the Earth to go to the afterlife – heaven or hell – without a burial ceremony. So Colley's ghost would haunt the spot where he was left to rot. Other ghosts were thought to be the spirits of people who had been murdered or who had died very suddenly.

Warding off ghosts

Colley's body, in its gibbet, was suspended at a crossroads. It was thought that his ghost would be confused by all the roads. Therefore, it would not be able to find its way back to take revenge on the people who had hanged him there.

His ghost is still said to haunt the place of the hanging. Recent stories say that his ghost now appears as a large black dog.

Types of ghost

Haunting Ghosts

▲ Haunting ghosts are seen at different times and by different people yet it is always the same ghost that appears in the same place. They seem to be totally unaware of living people. They are only attracted by the place which they haunt. Animals as well as people can be ghosts.

Ghosts of the living

▲ Strangely enough, many ghosts that are reported are of living people. The witness will suddenly see the ghost of a friend or relative, who is near death or in great trouble. Yet the person whose ghost it is may be many miles away. Such ghosts usually appear only once.

Purposeful ghosts

▲ Sometimes ghosts appear for a special reason. These ghosts are the phantoms of dead people appearing to give warnings or messages to the living, usually to family or close friends. The ghost rarely speaks, but it points or makes signs to deliver its message.

Duties of a ghost

Many legends tell of ghosts that appear because they have special tasks to carry out.

☠ Some ghosts return to avenge a murder and to expose the guilty villain.

☠ Other ghosts have to set right an injustice from which someone is still suffering. They make sure that money or property is returned to its rightful owner.

☠ Ghosts also come back to put right any wrongs they may have committed when alive.

☠ Sometimes ghosts appear to reveal the hiding place in which they hoarded money or treasure.

Poltergeists

Poltergeist activity is responsible for some rather alarming aspects of the supernatural, such as these cups and saucers flying through the air. Many people think that poltergeists are ghosts, but they do not behave like 'normal' ghosts.

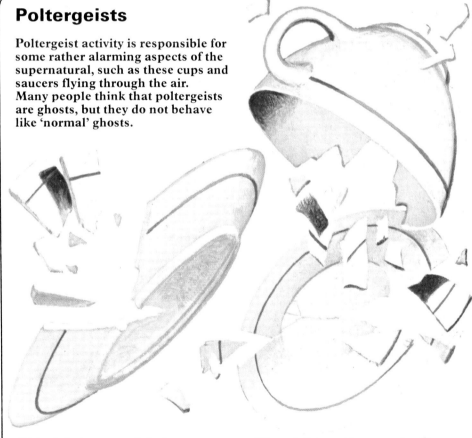

Objects being moved during poltergeist activity behave very oddly. They can be too hot to handle. They can move through doors or windows too small to let them through. And, most mysterious, they can suddenly appear in mid-air.

Poltergeist activity usually happens when people between the ages of 12 and 16 are present, although it is not known why. One theory supposes that their minds may generate the mysterious power needed. Researchers call this unknown power psychokinesis – PK – the ability to move objects without touching them. If they are correct and PK exists, then there are no ghosts involved, just the side-effects of PK energy.

Ghosts of long ago

The belief in ghosts is at least as old as recorded history. Stone Age people buried their dead in a way that suggests that they believed in ghosts: skeletons have been found that were weighed down with stones or bound hand and foot with cords. Perhaps this was to prevent the dead person's ghost from rising up and wandering.

The legends of the ancient Greeks and Romans are filled with phantoms of the dead. Greek ghosts seemed to interfere with the living more than ghosts in modern stories do. Most Greek ghosts were believed to be cruel, terrorizing people, causing trouble.

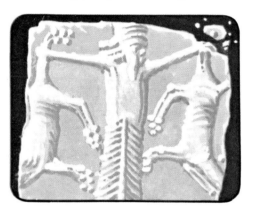

▲ The first record of a ghost comes from the Epic of Gilgamesh, an old Babylonian tale, written in 2,000 BC. The story is etched in clay tablets. It tells of the hero Gilgamesh and the ghost of his dead friend which appeared as a transparent shape.

▲ The ancient Egyptians believed that bird-headed ghosts, called khu, were spirits of the dead. These evil spectres were thought to spread disease among human beings and to be able to invade the bodies of animals, driving them into howling madness.

▲ Some Greek ghosts, like the one above, appeared in the form of evil, menacing phantoms. These smoky shapes were said to snort violently, breathing out black smoke and giving off a foul stench.

The haunted villa of Athens

Haunted houses are a common theme of many ghost stories. The earliest record of a haunted house is about 2,000 years old. The tale, described below, comes from ancient Greece.

At that time, a villa in Athens was said to be haunted. Every night a mournful spectre wandered through the villa, clanking and shaking the heavy prison manacles and iron chains that bound its hands and feet. The people who rented the villa were driven from it in terror, and one even died of fright.

House to rent – the ghost comes free

In desperation, the landlord of the villa was forced to lower the rent to next to nothing. The bargain price for which the house was being let came to the attention of a philosopher called Athenodorus. He looked at the house and was delighted to rent it for so little money, ghost or no ghost. Athenodorus was fascinated by the story of the haunting and wanted to discover what lay at the bottom of the mystery.

The ghost appears

The first evening after moving in, as Athenodorus sat quietly working, he was interrupted by the ominous sound of clattering chains. Acting as if nothing were wrong, he calmly carried on with his work. The noise grew louder. Then the grey-haired ghost of an old man came into the room, gesturing and signalling for Athenodorus to get up and follow. The philosopher continued to ignore the phantom. The ghost drew nearer until it was hovering right over him. Athenodorus still took no notice. Finally, the defeated spectre turned and went back the way it had come, vanishing at last in the courtyard. Athenodorus watched and saw exactly where it disappeared.

The ghost laid to rest

The next day he returned to the spot with a magistrate and some workmen who dug up the site. They unearthed a skeleton shackled to a mound of rusting chains. After the bones were buried in a cemetery, the haunting stopped. Neither the ghost nor its shackles were ever seen again.

▲ Roman history is full of ghost tales. In 44 BC Brutus, an army general, headed a plot to murder Julius Caesar. On March 15, he and his fellow conspirators stabbed Caesar to death. Not long afterwards Brutus was visited by a huge frightening phantom which claimed to be the ghost of his evil genius. When the spectre reappeared in Brutus' tent (shown above) the night before battle, its purpose became clear – the phantom was an omen of doom. Brutus lost the battle and killed himself afterwards.★

▲ Although the ancient Chinese had great respect for their dead ancestors and even held feasts in their honour, they were terrified of the spirits of murdered people which were considered to be evil. When a Chinese ghost like this appeared, it was thought to be dressed in the clothes it had worn when alive. Its arrival was impressive. First, it appeared as a shapeless cloud, out of which the head and feet emerged. Finally the body formed, surrounded by a glowing green cloud.

Spotting a ghost

There is no easy answer to the question 'What does a ghost look like?' Ghosts vary greatly in appearance; some are transparent shapes, some are dark shadowy figures, others look completely lifelike. But over the years, some general characteristics of ghosts have been noted which may help you to spot a ghost.

 A ghost often wears strange or old-fashioned clothes.

 A ghost almost never speaks, even if it is spoken to.

 A ghost may vanish into thin air, walk through a wall or through the air.

 A ghost may suddenly materialize in a locked room, so making an 'impossible' appearance.

★ In Shakespeare's play, the phantom is described as being that of Julius Caesar.

Strange customs

Ghosts usually inspire fear when they appear. Many people believe that ghosts are evil creatures which will harm living people.

In the past people invented all kinds of strange customs to protect themselves from ghosts. Many of these practices depended on the belief that ghosts still behaved in the same way that they had done during their life on Earth.

So people tried to frighten them with loud noises and fire, to outwit them with clever tricks or to chase them away with strange rituals.

Keeping lemures at bay

The Romans were careful to avoid lemures, supposedly the ghosts of people who had led evil lives. Special festivals were held every year in May to keep away the lemures. Even today it is considered bad luck to be married during that month.

Frightened of noise

During these celebrations, drums were pounded. The ghosts were supposed to be afraid of the noise and the din was thought to make them fly away in fright. Just to be sure, black beans, shown in the picture above, were also burnt by the side of graves. The Romans believed that the foul-smelling smoke of the beans would be certain to keep lemures away.

Outwitting a rhea's ghost

Rheas are big flightless birds, similar to ostriches, that live in South America. The Lengua indians of South America used to hunt rheas. But having killed a bird, the indians thought that the rhea's ghost would try to reclaim its body. To prevent this, the indians used a trick to outwit the rhea's ghost. They plucked the feathers from the dead body's chest, leaving them in piles along the way home. Whenever the pursuing ghost came across the feathers, it stopped to see whether the pile was its whole body or only a part. Thus, the hunters had time to hurry home safely. The ghost was too timid to enter their village.

Nailing down the afrit

▲ The Arabs of the Middle East lived in great fear of evil spirits. They were especially frightened of being haunted by the spirits of people who had been murdered. They believed that a phantom, called an afrit, would rise from the spot where the murdered person's blood had splashed to the ground. There was only one way to stop this happening. A new nail had to be hammered into the earth exactly on the spot where the killing had taken place. The picture above shows the bloodstain being nailed firmly to the ground.

Befriending the ghost of a bear

▲ A bear hunt was an important event for the Indian tribes of North America. Before setting out, they held long fasts and made sacrifices to the ghosts of bears that had been killed in former hunts. This was to make the hunt a success. When a bear was killed it was brought back to the village and treated as an honoured guest. A chief's bonnet was placed on its head and bowls of food were set before it. Then it was politely invited to eat. Only after this elaborate ceremony to appease the dead animal's ghost was the bear skinned and cooked.

Flogging the graveyard ghost

▲ In the 17th century, witch hunts were common, and the supernatural was firmly believed in by people of every country. In south west England, a Reverend Dodge made a great name for himself as a fierce ghost-hunter. He would run along roads with a whip, shouting and flogging unseen spirits. He also lurked in churchyards, waiting to trap unwary ghosts. Whether he actually saw any is unproved, but according to one story, a ghost that he came across was so frightened that it gave out a loud cry and vanished forever.

Where ghosts gather

Ghosts are supposed to haunt the scene of death. It is therefore not surprising that many ghosts are reported at sites where death or violence on a large scale once took place.

You might expect the scene of a crash to be haunted by the same number of ghosts as those who died in it. But this is not always the case. It seems that for some unknown reason, only certain victims become ghosts.

Not everyone can see a ghost. Those who are able to do so are described as having psychic powers.

Ghosts on battlefields

An obvious place for a haunting ought to be a battlefield and a number of them are thought to harbour ghosts. Those that do so include Marathon in Greece, Waterloo in Belgium and Dunkirk in France.

Civil War phantoms

Shiloh in Tennessee, USA, is claimed to be haunted to this day. The Battle of Shiloh was a major conflict of the American Civil War. Two days of savage fighting in April, 1862 resulted in the deaths of over 24,000 men.

In the months that followed, stories of a phantom battle began to be told. The reports claimed that gunfire, the clashing of sabres and bayonets and the screams and shouts of dying men could be heard at the site of the battle. The picture on the right shows an impression of the phantom battle in action.

▲ Traditionally, the elm was a good tree from which to hang criminals. Its strong lower branches were ideal for suspending a noose. Elms are sometimes reputed to be haunted by the ghosts of the people who met an untimely end under their branches.

▲ A graveyard seems the natural place to find lots of ghosts. But this is not the case, as people rarely die in the graveyard itself. Ghosts normally haunt the place of death. Just one ghost is thought to exist in a graveyard. It is the 'graveyard guardian', the spirit of the first person to have been buried there. The guardian's task is to keep away evil spirits and unwanted intruders. An ancient ritual in Western Europe was to sacrifice a living person when a new burial ground was established, to make sure that it would have its guardian.

▲ There are many cases of people seeing and hearing the spirits of disaster victims, both before and after the event. The flaming crash of the R101 airship (shown above), was relived by a woman medium who was 'contacted' by the airship's captain. The airship had crashed in France two days earlier. The captain's voice, speaking through the medium, described the last moments of the flight. Its description proved to be accurate, as an official enquiry later showed. Perhaps this is a true contact from beyond the grave.

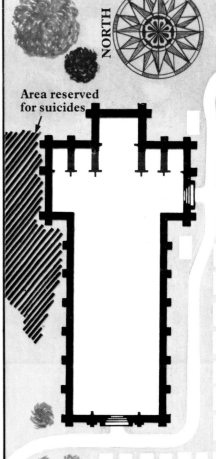

A special burial place

Until the late 19th century, the north side of a church graveyard (shown in black on the plan view below), was rarely used to bury people in. It was the part of the churchyard often cast in gloom and shadow.

NORTH

Area reserved for suicides

The custom came from old Germanic beliefs. The area was suitable only for the restless souls (and possibly restless ghosts) of those who had committed suicide, which was considered an unpardonable sin. Suicides were also buried at crossroads. A stake was driven through their hearts, to stop a ghost from appearing at the spot. Even if it did, like Tom Colley's ghost, it would be confused by the four roads and stay in the same place until it faded away.

Phantoms of the sea

In the days of sailing ships, crews were often out of sight of land for weeks on end. Alone at sea, sailors had to face the perils of uncharted islands and reefs, sudden storms and freak giant waves. Sometimes ships disappeared and were never seen again. It is no wonder that sailors became famous for their superstitions and ghost stories.

Over the years, scores of phantom ships have been reported, gliding mysteriously across the waves. Ships that had ghosts as 'passengers' were thought to be jinxed – to have bad luck. A jinxed ship was doomed to encounter terrible disaster.

Captain Kidd's ghost

In 1701, the famous pirate leader Captain Kidd was captured and sentenced to death. He was hanged, then his dead body, shown on the right, was put in a gibbet as a warning to other pirates.

Like most pirate leaders, Captain Kidd buried his gold treasure. Then he killed the men who helped him bury it and left their ghosts to guard it. Years later, treasure hunters, digging for the loot, struck an iron chest. The chest instantly sank out of sight. A pirate ghost was supposed to have jumped out of the hole and attacked the men, driving them away in shrieking terror.

The unluckiest ship afloat

In 1858, the *Great Eastern* was the largest passenger ship in the world. Yet from the start, it was thought that the ship was jinxed. Several people were killed while building it and one workman, a riveter, vanished mysteriously as he hammered away in the hull. The ship's launching was a bad omen too. The ship stuck fast on the slip, and it was months before it floated free.

Launched at last

Only a few hours after steaming out to sea, one of the funnels blew up, killing six of the crew. During the first crossing the passengers were disturbed by the dull thuds of hammering from below. Then came a a terrible storm, during which the giant paddle wheels were ripped away from the sides of the ship. The crew panicked and refused to obey the captain's orders. The *Great Eastern* survived, but it never worked as a liner again, being used for laying telegraph cables. In 1885, the ship was towed to a breaker's yard. As the workers tore into the hull, they found the remains of the riveter who had been sealed in alive nearly 30 years before. Could it have been the sound of his ghostly hammering that had echoed throughout the ship's career?

▶ The *Great Eastern* had a double hull with one metre gap between the two sections. This was where the skeleton of the missing riveter and his bag of rusty tools were found.

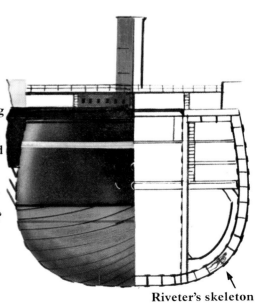

Riveter's skeleton

The haunted submarine

Many ghost stories have their origins in the strange events that occur during wartime. One of the most bizarre is about the haunted German submarine, the UB-65.

The UB-65 was built in 1916 during World War 1. During its construction, a series of accidents killed five men and injured several others. Although the submarine crew was highly superstitious and reluctant to sail, the ship was needed badly, and so it was launched despite the ominous signs of impending doom.

A near disaster

During the preparations for the submarine's first dive, a sailor threw himself over the side without warning. The captain continued the mission as if nothing had happened. But when he tried to surface, the UB-65 would not rise. Sea water began seeping into the ship, soon reaching the batteries and causing them to give off deadly fumes. At last, the desperate captain managed to surface with his crew almost dead from suffocation.

The phantom lieutenant

Back in port, the UB-65 was loading supplies when a torpedo exploded, killing six men including a lieutenant. Shortly after, a terrified petty officer and another sailor claimed the ghost of the dead lieutenant had come aboard. A few weeks later, while patrolling off the English coast, the ghost was spotted standing in the bows. The phantom appeared once more as the ship put into port. A few moments later the captain was killed as enemy planes attacked the harbour.

A chaplain was summoned to drive away, or exorcise, the ghost. For the next few months, the UB-65 functioned normally. Then suddenly the chief gunner went mad and killed himself, and the day after that, the petty officer jumped over the side. In the next battle the ship was hit. The lights inside the submarine flashed wildly, and an eerie green glow filled the hull. Once more the damaged UB-65 limped back to port.

The final sighting

Late in the war, an American ship came across a strange sight. The crew saw the UB-65 abandoned and drifting at sea. Suddenly an explosion tore through the submarine. Before it slid under, the figure of the ghostly officer appeared for the last time.

Unlikely ghosts

Ghosts are normally phantoms of either living or dead people. But ghosts of animals and even of objects have been seen. There are countless tales of phantom fire-breathing horses galloping through the night.

Ghosts do not have to be of living things. Tales of phantom ships have been told for centuries, and today there are stories of ghostly cars, buses and aeroplanes.

In the future, there will probably be stories of phantom spaceships, astronauts, and perhaps of strange creatures on other worlds.

▲ The phantom machine shown above is the ghost of a Spitfire fighter plane. The howling sound of its engine is said to be heard as it flies a low victory roll over its former airfield, the World War 2 airbase of Biggin Hill, England.

1 The talking mongoose

One of the most bizarre hauntings on record is that of a talking mongoose named Gef. Haunting ghosts almost never speak to people. Certainly animal ghosts are not supposed to – yet Gef the mongoose not only spoke but also told jokes and stories, swore and sang songs.

Nobody could make out just what Gef actually was. He was not a poltergeist at work; nor did he seem to be an hallucination or a hoax. He simply claimed that he was a ghost in the form of a small mongoose.

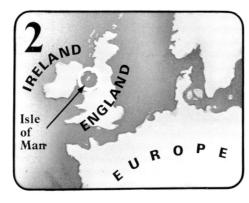

▲ The Isle of Man lies between Ireland and England. It is supposedly a centre of witchcraft, and it is also said to be heavily haunted. In the 1930s, a mysterious talking mongoose appeared on the island near its west coast town of Dalby.

▲ The talking mongoose, who said his name was Gef, haunted an old seaside farmhouse. The first signs of him appeared when the owners began to see a shadow prowling about the house nibbling food, rattling saucers and, for some reason, blowing out candles.

The phantom hound

For centuries, huge phantom dogs have cropped up in ghost legends. They are known all over northern Europe and in parts of North America.

At night demon dogs haunted lonely country roads, graveyards and old gallows sites. According to legend, anyone who saw a phantom hound would soon be stricken with disaster or death. Luckily, these dogs left people alone unless provoked.

Black Shuck

One of the dogs, shown here, was known as Black Shuck. It was supposed to be an enormous beast, the size of a calf. Its shaggy coat was as black as soot. One of the things that made Black Shuck different from other ghostly dogs was its eye. This was a single cyclops-eye, as large as a saucer, in the centre of its forehead. The dog had a fiendish howl. Foam and fire dripped from its jaws and its breath blew like a strong gust of wind.

The ghostly lift

In 1969, a large rambling seaside hotel in Wales was awaiting demolition. But before the demolition crew could arrive, a number of strange things took place as if the old hotel were pro- testing against its undignified end.

The main mystery was the lift that began to move by itself. Without warning, it would rise from the ground floor to the second floor and stop. This should have been impossible as the electricity had been switched off weeks before. Eventually, the lift's cables were cut, but even that did not stop it. Workmen had to climb into the shaft and pound the lift with sledge hammers before it finally crashed to the bottom of its shaft.

▲ One day, the owner of the house saw a pair of furry paws poke out from a crack in the ceiling. She tried to touch them but instead was bitten. Then a high shrill voice, speaking in excellent English, told her to go and put ointment on the bite.

▲ Gef became famous and was featured in many newspaper stories. But he has not made an appearance for many years. The farmhouse was sold and the new owners reported having shot a strange little animal in the grounds. Could this have been Gef?

The haunted house

Many ghosts haunt one particular place such as the house where they once lived. These haunting spirits are seen time and time again, wandering through the house.

Haunting ghosts are thought to occur because of a violent or dramatic event in the past which links a spirit to a place. Houses where a brutal crime was committed or someone was bitterly unhappy are often haunted.

Some of the strange noises which make people think a house is haunted are caused by natural events, such as the creaking of shrinking and expanding timbers or the sound of rats and mice scurrying about.

Inside the house

Many strange things can occur in a haunted house. Here are some of them. The numbers below link with the numbers on the picture.

1   A ghostly figure glides from room to room passing straight through solid walls.
2   The curtains in a closed room start swaying in a mysterious breeze.
3   A skeleton is found walled up inside a hidden secret room.
4   The ghost of a member of the family materializes in front of its own, suddenly blank portrait.
5   Muddy footprints appear on the stairway as the thud of slow heavy footsteps is heard.
6   In the attic, objects move and fall to the floor while strange thumpings and bangings are heard.
7   An old skull screams whenever it is moved from the house to be buried.
8   A grandfather clock chimes thirteen, foretelling a death in the family.
9   A bloodstain on the floor cannot be removed. No matter how many times it is washed away, it always returns.
10   Groaning sounds come from a secret, cobweb-choked passage which leads from the fireplace to an upstairs room.
11   A pair of white-gloved hands appears at the piano and begins to play a funeral march.
12   Unseen forces set a chandelier swaying so violently that pieces of crystal crash to the floor.

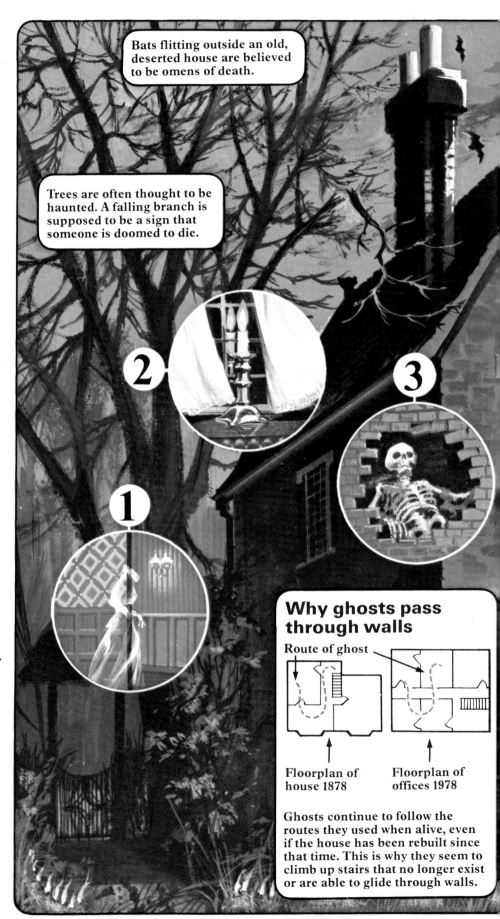

Bats flitting outside an old, deserted house are believed to be omens of death.

Trees are often thought to be haunted. A falling branch is supposed to be a sign that someone is doomed to die.

Why ghosts pass through walls

Route of ghost

Floorplan of house 1878

Floorplan of offices 1978

Ghosts continue to follow the routes they used when alive, even if the house has been rebuilt since that time. This is why they seem to climb up stairs that no longer exist or are able to glide through walls.

The sudden hoot of an owl is a warning that death is about to strike.

Corpse lights are small flames flickering just above the ground. Especially common in graveyards, they are said to show the way that a funeral procession will soon pass.

HAUNTED PLACES
The village with a dozen ghosts

Some places have a reputation for being particularly haunted. The village of Pluckley in south-east England is one of these. It is claimed to have no fewer than 12 ghosts.

The villagers do not agree as to whether the ghosts exist, but it seems unlikely that the village should get its reputation for no reason at all.

Researchers point out that conflicting opinions about ghosts can be a sign that they really do exist. If everyone had the same opinion, it would probably mean that they had read the same book or newspaper report.

The photographs on this page were taken recently. There were no signs of supernatural activity when the photographer took the pictures, and as you can see, no phantoms appeared on them.

The colonel of the woods

Park Wood was formerly a small stretch of forested ground on the outskirts of Pluckley. In recent times, it was cleared to become grazing land as you can see from the picture above. A colonel once hanged himself in the woods and his ghost used to be seen walking in them.

The hanging body of the schoolmaster

Soon after World War 1, a schoolmaster committed suicide in the village. He hanged himself from a laurel tree that stood in the road once known as Dicky Buss's Lane. His phantom body is said to be visible to this day, swinging in the breeze.

The spectre of the highwayman

The ghost of a highwayman haunts the area where a hollow oak tree stood at Fright Corner. Here the man was ambushed by his enemies. He was run through with a sword and speared to the tree. The gory event is said to be re-enacted every night.

The Pinnock

Fright Corner

A phantom coach and horses

The road from Pluckley to nearby Maltman's Hill is haunted by a phantom coach drawn by four horses. On dark nights it is supposed to be possible to hear the drumming of horses' hooves and the sound of the coach rumbling along the lonely road.

The ghost of the gypsy woman

The spectre of a pipe-smoking gypsy woman, huddled in a tattered shawl, is often claimed to be visible near the bridge by the crossroads. She was burned to death in mysterious circumstances and has haunted the site ever since.

The black ghost of the miller

Near a house called The Pinnock is an old ruined mill where the black shape of a miller's ghost is said to wander. The ghost only appears before a thunderstorm breaks over the village.

Clay-pit and brickworks

Pluckley railway station

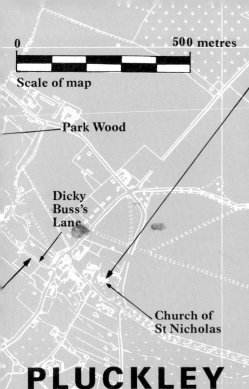

0   500 metres

Scale of map

Park Wood

Dicky
Buss's
Lane

Church of
St Nicholas

PLUCKLEY

Greystones

Rose Court

The Red Lady and a mysterious modern ghost

The Church of St Nicholas, left, is said to be haunted by the ghost of the beautiful Lady Dering who died in the 12th century. She was buried in a sumptuous gown with a red rose in her hands. Her body was placed inside seven lead coffins, one inside the other, which were then put into an oak casket that was buried in a vault under the church. To this day her ghost, known as the Red Lady, walks in the graveyard of the church. Recently, there have also been reports of another mysterious female figure wandering inside the church, above right. She may be Pluckley's newest ghost.

Surrenden
Dering

The White Lady of Dering

Surrenden Dering was the manor of the Dering family. The main house was burnt by a fire in 1952. The house was supposed to have been haunted for centuries by the ghost of another member of the family, known as the White Lady, who appeared gliding through the library.

NORTH

The ghost of the screaming man

Near the railway station is a clay-pit and a brickworks. A worker was smothered to death when a wall of clay fell on him. His ghost, which is said to haunt the site, screams in the same way as he did when he died.

The Lady of Rose Court

The house known as Rose Court is supposed to be haunted by the spirit of a former owner. She killed herself by drinking the juices of crushed poisonous berries. Her ghost appears between four and five o'clock in the afternoon, the time of day when she died.

The phantom monk

At a house called Greystones, a phantom monk is said to haunt the grounds. He is often seen with the lady of Rose Court. There seems to have been a mysterious connection between the two of them for she died by a window, looking towards Greystones.

Ghosts around the world

Ghost stories and legends occur in countries all over the world.

The spirits come in all shapes and sizes. They behave in many different ways, mainly based on the customs of the area which they are thought to haunt.

Many of the ghosts are created by people's imagination. But one question remains unanswered – if ghosts do not exist, why should so many stories have been invented about them?

These pages show you just a few of the phantoms which, perhaps, haunt the Earth.

To Mexico

SOUTH AMERICA

NORTH AMERICA

EUROPE

AFRICA

The railway ghost

There is an American legend that claims that the ghostly funeral train shown here of President Abraham Lincoln still rumbles along the railway track in New York State, more than 100 years after his death.

The glowing ghost

This ghostly apparition seemed to foretell the death of Roderigo Borgia in 15th century Italy. Minutes after the glowing ghost was seen, Borgia fell screaming to the ground, dying from the poisoned wine that he had drunk.

The bandit ghost

In Mexico, ghosts of people who had died violently were said to be able to cure illness. The ghost of the famous bandit, Pancho Villa, cured an insane boy by whipping and shouting to drive out the evil spirits thought to possess him.

The slave ghost

In southern Africa, people believed that if a witch doctor dug up a corpse and stole part of the body, he could turn its ghost into a slave. Then the witch doctor sent the ghost out to do his evil deeds – to spread sickness and kill his enemies.

The legless ghost

Japanese ghosts were believed to be deformed as a punishment for evil deeds when alive. Many were legless, their lower limbs engulfed in flames. According to legend, they warned people when death was near.

The eating ghost

The people of the Banks Islands in the Pacific Ocean believed that certain stones were haunted by 'eating ghosts'. If a person's shadow fell across such a stone the ghost was thought to suck out the person's soul. After losing his soul, the person died. These stones were placed in empty houses to keep away thieves.

PACIFIC OCEAN

A S I A

INDIA

AUSTRALIA

The gibbering ghost

Indians believed in ghosts called bauta. They were hideous creatures with small, red bodies and huge, lion-like teeth. They gibbered through their noses when they spoke. They were supposed to roam at night, attacking people.

The waterfall ghost

In 1905, two men on holiday saw a pair of ghostly hands come out of a waterfall. The hands beckoned to them. Looking behind the waterfall, they found a cave with three skeletons in it. The ghostly presence had fulfilled its task–to draw attention to the remains of of the dead.

Ghost hunting

Many people claim to have seen ghosts, but very few can offer any kind of proof.

Professional ghost hunters, called psychic researchers, are brought in to examine places which are thought to be haunted.

Although the investigators may have lots of scientific equipment to study any supernatural happenings, investigating ghosts is not easy.

Usually the investigators work with second-hand evidence and reports from witnesses. They must also try to discover whether the 'ghost' is a fake or whether it was caused by some natural event.

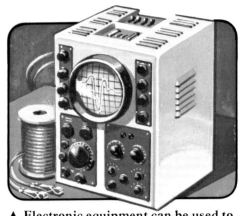

▲ Electronic equipment can be used to measure temperature and humidity and to detect the draughts and vibrations associated with ghosts. However, some investigators claim that their electronic gear (shown above) can even detect the 'psychic energy' of ghosts.

▲ A thin layer of flour or powder brushed on floors, ledges and stairways will show up any footprints or fingerprints made by fake 'ghosts'. Flour can also be dusted around furniture and other objects to reveal whether they have been moved.

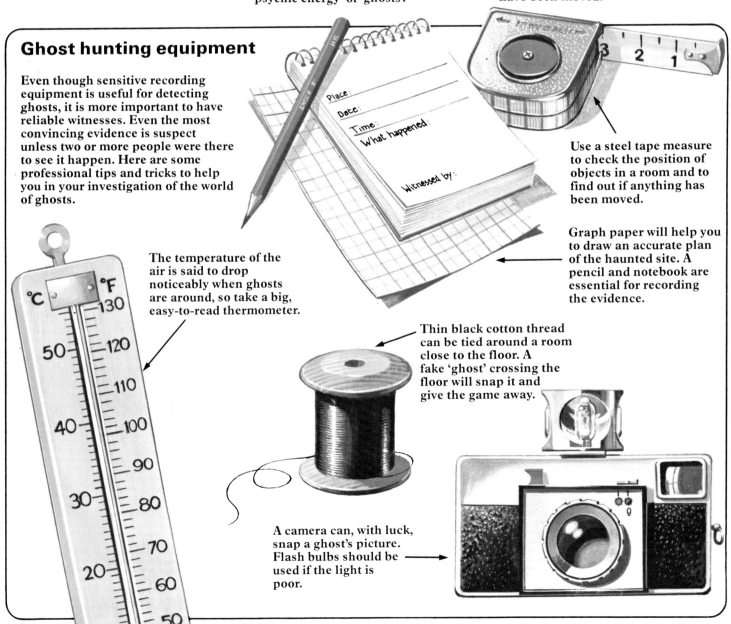

Ghost hunting equipment

Even though sensitive recording equipment is useful for detecting ghosts, it is more important to have reliable witnesses. Even the most convincing evidence is suspect unless two or more people were there to see it happen. Here are some professional tips and tricks to help you in your investigation of the world of ghosts.

Use a steel tape measure to check the position of objects in a room and to find out if anything has been moved.

Graph paper will help you to draw an accurate plan of the haunted site. A pencil and notebook are essential for recording the evidence.

The temperature of the air is said to drop noticeably when ghosts are around, so take a big, easy-to-read thermometer.

Thin black cotton thread can be tied around a room close to the floor. A fake 'ghost' crossing the floor will snap it and give the game away.

A camera can, with luck, snap a ghost's picture. Flash bulbs should be used if the light is poor.

Professional ghost hunting

A psychic researcher was called in to investigate a house where three people had reported strange events which made them believe the house was haunted.

The researcher arranged to spend the night in the room in which the ghost had appeared. He took with him a trunk of equipment to detect and record everything that happened.

Setting up the equipment

On arrival, the first thing the researcher did was to question the occupants about what they had seen and heard. Then he prepared the room for the night.

First the door and window were sealed shut with tape. A length of thread was placed all around the room so that anything brushing against it would set off a camera loaded with infra-red film, which could take photographs in the dark.

The researcher also put into position a draught-measuring device and a heat-sensitive switch which would set off the camera if the temperature changed. Beside the bed he placed a normal flash-equipped camera and a tape recorder.

Lastly, he ran a hearing aid from the infra-red camera to the bed so that he could hear it click from where he slept. A recording thermometer and a barometer were also set working.

The end of the investigation

The night passed quietly. Even with the carefully prepared traps, however, there was not the slightest sign of a ghost. Once again, a phantom had refused to co-operate.

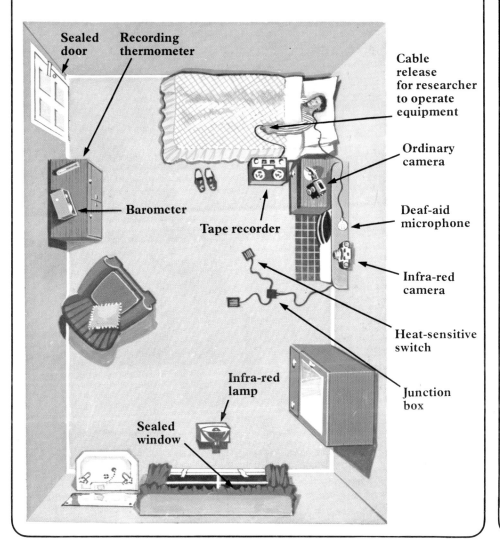

- Sealed door
- Recording thermometer
- Cable release for researcher to operate equipment
- Ordinary camera
- Barometer
- Tape recorder
- Deaf-aid microphone
- Infra-red camera
- Heat-sensitive switch
- Junction box
- Infra-red lamp
- Sealed window

Animal investigators

Some animals are known to be more aware of ghosts than people. They can be curiously sensitive to the strange atmosphere that lingers in haunted places. For this reason, investigators sometimes use animals to look for ghosts.

An American ghost hunter, investigating a house in Kentucky that was supposed to have a haunted room, took with him a rat, a cat, a dog and a rattlesnake. The animals were put into the haunted room one at a time.

The rat behaved normally, but the other animals all reacted in a surprising way. The rattlesnake at once reared up to strike an empty chair in the room. When the cat was carried into the room, it leapt to the floor and hissed and glowered at the same empty chair. The dog ran from the room snarling. It refused to go back.

Later, when the animals were tested in another room, they all behaved normally. The ghost hunter concluded that the animals could sense a ghostly presence in the haunted room which could not be sensed by human beings.

Ghost stories explained

Many ghost stories turn out to be untrue once psychic researchers look into them. Often they find that the signs which people took to be a ghost have a perfectly ordinary explanation.

It is not hard to understand why peoples in the past believed in ghosts as there was little scientific knowledge of how natural events were caused.

Today, investigators often find that people are actually disappointed rather than pleased when they are told that a 'ghost' was just the wind or flowing water. It seems that people would prefer to believe in ghosts.

Knockings at Netherfield

In 1946, a front page story in a newspaper caught the attention of two psychic researchers. The story was about a house that was filled with strange noises. It was thought that the house was haunted.

When the researchers arrived on the scene, they were told that hollow knocking sounds had been heard coming from the kitchen ceiling for several years. The researchers decided to spend the night in the house but first they checked the bedroom above for possible natural causes. Finding an alarm clock on a bedside chair, they took it downstairs with them.

That night faint knocking sounds came from the kitchen itself. The investigators traced the sound to the clock. Taking it apart, they found that the tightly wound spring was unwinding in jerks and making the faintest of tapping sounds.

The ghost revealed

The tapping noise itself was barely noticeable. But when the clock stood upstairs on the bedside chair, the noises it made passed down the chair legs, through the floor and were amplified to a loud knocking by the very thin plaster of the kitchen ceiling. So the 'ghost' was an alarm clock.

1 Ghosts from under the ground

This true story shows how unseen events can convince even the most sceptical people that ghosts are present.

The rumblings and noises that shook the house were investigated by lots of people, yet they did not find what was causing the 'haunting'. Although, as you will see, the cause proved to be a natural one, it is not surprising that it remained hidden until psychic researchers conducted a thorough investigation.

▲ In the 1950s, a house in Yorkshire, England, was invaded by mysterious eerie noises. Explosions and the sounds of banging, as if doors were being slammed, continued over a period of some months. The loudest noises literally shook the walls of the house.

▲ The two doctors who used the house as a surgery called in a plumber to inspect the water pipes. They also had the gas and electrical systems examined. Even the police came to inspect the house. But no-one could find a reason for the noises.

▲ The research team went outside to examine the foundations of the house. They found an old sewer, no longer used, in the garden, where earlier the ground had sunk but had since been filled in. The sewer passed very near the house, but it was choked with dirt and earth.

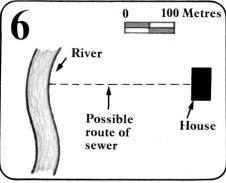

0   100 Metres

River

Possible route of sewer

House

▲ They could not crawl along the sewer, but its direction showed that it emptied into a nearby river. The river was tidal – its level went up and down depending on the sea. The researchers hunted for the sewer's outlet along the banks of the river but without success.

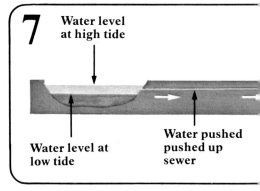

Water level at high tide

Water level at low tide

Water pushed pushed up sewer

▲ The diagram above shows a cross-section through the soil between the house and the river. The researchers found that high tides were forcing water up the sewer, and despite its semi-blocked state, water was seeping through the soil under the house. The

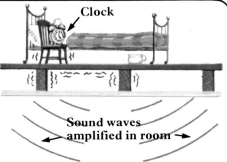

Clock

Sound waves amplified in room →

▲ This diagram shows how the clock spring's tapping turned into a ghostly knocking. The vibration passed down the legs of the bedside chair, then through the floor and the joists. The thin plaster ceiling amplified the vibrations into the room below.

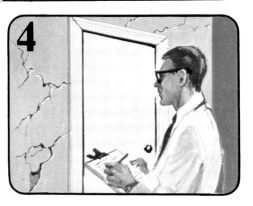

4

▲ The doctors, wondering if the house were haunted, asked a team of psychic researchers to investigate. The team noticed cracks in the walls, badly fitting doors and a dip in the roof. These all seemed to be signs that the house was moving on its foundations.

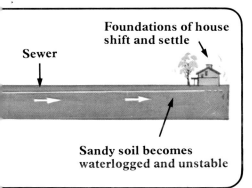

Foundations of house shift and settle →

Sewer

Sandy soil becomes waterlogged and unstable

foundations of the house were settling, and the movements were causing the noises that had been heard. The final proof was that the noises were loudest when the tide was at its highest. So the psychic researchers recorded it as yet another 'haunting' with a natural cause.

Spectres of the Brocken

For centuries people have reported seeing huge ghostly figures haunting the Harz mountains in West Germany. It was believed that these ghosts gathered together once a year in May on the summit of the Brocken, the highest mountain in the region.

However, less than a century ago this ghost legend was shown to have a natural explanation. It was people's imaginations that had turned it into a ghost story.

It turned out that the phantoms of the Brocken were nothing more than the shadows of climbers that had been cast onto clouds swirling around the peak. The climbers had to be on or near the summit, and the weather conditions had to be just right for the 'ghosts' to appear.

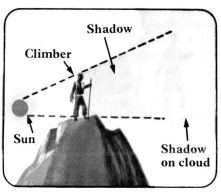

Shadow

Climber

Sun

Shadow on cloud

▲ Ghostly figures were seen around the Brocken when the sun was setting and a bank of light cloud hung around the summit. Climbers' shadows projected onto the clouds could be as much as 200 metres high.

Clever fakes

Some ghosts cannot be explained by natural physical causes, or even by supernatural ones. When they are investigated they are found to be the work of human beings. In other words, they are fakes.

Convincing people that a fake ghost is real is not very hard. Most people are quite willing to accept that mysterious forces exist which cannot be explained.

Fake ghosts have been used to play upon people's natural fears and suspicions for all kinds of reasons. They have been invented to keep secrets hidden, to cover up murders and to cheat people out of their money.

▲ Smugglers, a few hundred years ago, were well known for using ghost legends to their own advantage when they made their illegal runs.

One smuggler cleverly gave new life to an old tale about a ghost carriage and a headless horse. He painted his horse white, except for its head. On the carriage which he used to carry his smuggled goods, the smuggler hung a set of lights. Anyone who met him at night would swear to having seen a headless horse pulling a glowing phantom carriage.

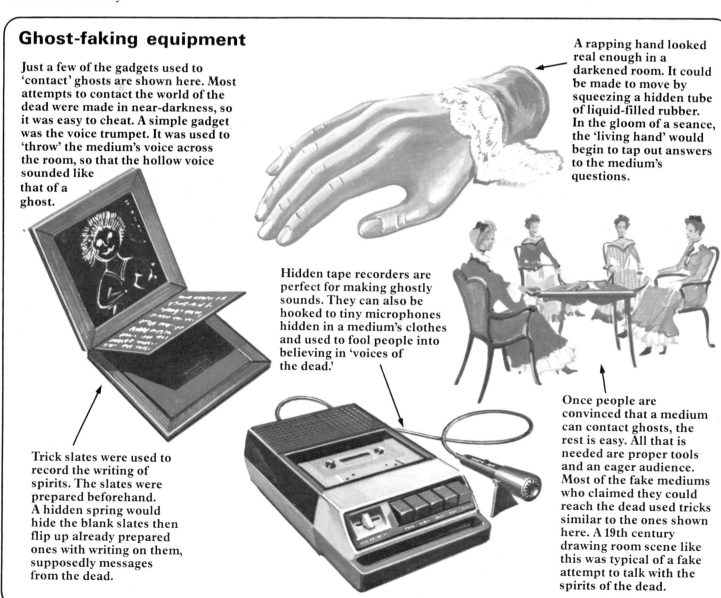

Ghost-faking equipment

Just a few of the gadgets used to 'contact' ghosts are shown here. Most attempts to contact the world of the dead were made in near-darkness, so it was easy to cheat. A simple gadget was the voice trumpet. It was used to 'throw' the medium's voice across the room, so that the hollow voice sounded like that of a ghost.

A rapping hand looked real enough in a darkened room. It could be made to move by squeezing a hidden tube of liquid-filled rubber. In the gloom of a seance, the 'living hand' would begin to tap out answers to the medium's questions.

Hidden tape recorders are perfect for making ghostly sounds. They can also be hooked to tiny microphones hidden in a medium's clothes and used to fool people into believing in 'voices of the dead.'

Once people are convinced that a medium can contact ghosts, the rest is easy. All that is needed are proper tools and an eager audience. Most of the fake mediums who claimed they could reach the dead used tricks similar to the ones shown here. A 19th century drawing room scene like this was typical of a fake attempt to talk with the spirits of the dead.

Trick slates were used to record the writing of spirits. The slates were prepared beforehand. A hidden spring would hide the blank slates then flip up already prepared ones with writing on them, supposedly messages from the dead.

Photographs of the dead

Spirit photographs were a tremendous craze in the late 19th century. Photography was then a new technology and most people believed that it was impossible to trick a camera. Photographers were flooded with requests to have pictures taken with ghosts of the dead.

Spirit photography became a great opportunity for frauds and cheats. By using photographic tricks and by tampering with film in the darkroom, spirit pictures were easy to make. Investigations revealed that in most cases the 'ghost' was a dummy, a

▲ The pictures in the left hand column above are examples of the sort of fake spirits that could be conjured up by a good photographer. In the right hand column is a sequence which has not been proved to be a fake. Taken in the 1930s, the pictures shown an Indian girl, Silver Belle, appearing in front of a medium. The audience of 81 people who watched the figure emerge found no evidence of cheating.

cardboard doll or a dressed-up assistant. So many photographs proved to be fakes that the public stopped believing in them altogether.

Sense or nonsense?

Many people are convinced that they have seen ghosts. But do ghosts really exist? Unfortunately the evidence gathered is not always reliable. Many accounts of ghosts are so far-fetched that they are obviously nonsense or outright fakes. Many other ghosts have been shown to be the result of odd light conditions playing tricks on the eyes.

There have been a number of attempts to explain ghosts. But the theories do not account for all aspects of ghostly behaviour. As the pictures opposite show, some evidence for ghosts is still unexplainable.

Who believes in ghosts?

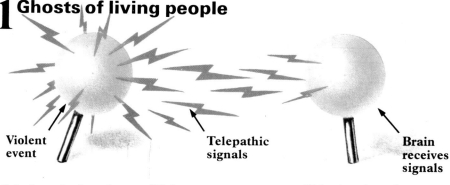

People interviewed — People who had seen ghosts — Types of ghost seen

1,684

615 — Living
275 — Dead
639 — Unknown
155 — Other

17,000

These ghosts were recognized by the people who saw them

One of the first tasks undertaken by researchers was to find out how many people claimed to have seen ghosts.

In 1890, they completed a survey which was carried out in several European countries. 17,000 people were questioned, and their answers are shown in the chart above. Studies which have been carried out since then have all shown similar results.

Two types of ghost

Modern theories of ghosts reject the idea that they are literally the 'spirits' of people.

Ghosts of the living are thought to be linked with telepathy. This is the name given to the mysterious (and unproven) ability of some people to send or receive messages without using physical methods. The brain is thought to interpret a telepathic signal as a visual image, or 'ghost'.

Ghosts of the dead are thought to be 'psychic images'. They were formed as the result of an extreme emotional event.

1 Ghosts of living people

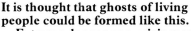

Violent event

Telepathic signals

Brain receives signals

It is thought that ghosts of living people could be formed like this.

Extreme danger or a crisis may cause the brain to send out telepathic thought signals, rather like a radio sending out an emergency SOS message. This signal can be received by the brain of a sensitive person, as the brain 'tunes in' to the SOS message. The brain interprets the signal as a picture, so it is thought to be a ghost.

2 Ghosts of the dead

A — Violent event

B — Psychic image formed

C — Image absorbs energy

D — Image remains for many years

E — Image fades away

Haunting ghosts (though not purposeful ghosts, which remain unexplained) are thought to be formed like this.

When a violent event occurs, such as a murder, an unknown force is generated to form a 'psychic image' at the spot where the death happened. The invisible image continues to exist by absorbing energy (such as heat) from the surrounding air. This could explain why the area of a haunting is usually cold.

The image survives for many years as a faithful record of the original event. It can be seen by people who are sensitive to the psychic forces which created it. Gradually however, it fades away, becoming fainter and fainter until it vanishes completely.

Mystery photographs

People believe photographs because cameras 'do not lie'. Yet the spirit pictures that were once all the rage were nearly all shown to be faked.

But photographs of ghosts that have not been tampered with at all are the hardest to understand. Although they are the best proof yet gathered that ghosts do exist, they raise more questions than they answer. If ghosts really are psychic images, then how can ordinary photographic film record them? Yet all three of these pictures are considered by experts to be genuine.

▲ The ghost of Raynham Hall was claimed to have the shape of a woman. In 1936 came startling proof.
A photographer was setting up his equipment at the foot of the stairs. He saw a phantom drifting down them and hastily took the picture shown above.

▲ People commonly claim to see the ghosts of nuns and priests in churches. Often they are said to stand at or near the altar, praying. The photograph above of a cowled monk standing by an altar rail was taken in the early 1960s by the vicar of a church in England.

At the time he saw nothing that was out of the ordinary. But his developed film showed the tall phantom monk seen here. It appears to be about three metres tall. The film was carefully checked by photographic experts but showed no signs of tampering.

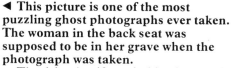

◄ This picture is one of the most puzzling ghost photographs ever taken. The woman in the back seat was supposed to be in her grave when the photograph was taken.

The driver's wife took this picture of her husband sitting in the car. She claims that there was nobody in the car except her husband. Yet the photograph clearly shows the figure of a woman – her mother – who had died a week before.

Experts say that the film has not been altered in any way. Yet if you look closely you will see that the corner of her scarf seems to overlap the side pillar of the car. This would only be possible if her face was placed in the picture after it was taken. Yet if the experts are correct and the photograph is genuine, there is no explanation for how it could have happened – unless the woman in the back was a ghost.

A dictionary of ghostlore

This dictionary of ghosts, ghostly events and related topics includes many of the subjects that have appeared in this book as well as some that are new. Together they make up only a very small part of the world of the unknown.

AFTERLIFE The place to which the human soul is believed to go after the body dies. Many people believe that a soul in the afterlife can contact the living, although it does not haunt the Earth.

APPARITION This is the term used by professional ghost researchers to describe all kinds of ghosts no matter whether they are human, animal or objects.

Artificial ghosts

Magicians of the Middle Ages tried all sorts of ways to contact the dead. Many French alchemists thought they could create ghosts out of human blood. They carried out experiments with heating samples of blood in charcoal burners like the one above. A number of doubtful reports claim that ghostly shapes really did appear in the clouds of steam.

Doppelganger

Also known as a fetch, this ghost is supposed to be the double of a living human being. If people are unfortunate enough to see their own doppelganger, it can be an omen that they will die in the near future.

ESP These initials stand for Extra Sensory Perception. Sight, sound, smell, touch, taste are the five known human senses. Other possible senses such as telepathy or psychokinesis are classed as ESP.

EXORCISM A ritual usually performed by a priest to drive out a spirit from the place it is haunting.

FADING GHOSTS A haunting ghost often fades away with time. But there are stories of ghosts of Roman legionaries which have been haunting for at least 1,600 years.

GHOST DANCE Ceremony performed by the Plains Indians of North America in the late 19th century. The dance was performed by Indians wearing 'ghost shirts'. The Indians thought that spirits would help them drive the white settlers from their territory.

GHOUL An especially nasty and evil-looking kind of spirit. Ghouls are supposed to feed on the dead.

Fake ghosts

One of the cleverest tricks of the 19th century was to bring a phantom onto a stage. A large sheet of glass was angled in front of a ghost-playing actor who was hidden below the stage. The actor's brightly lit image was reflected onto the glass. But to the audience, the ghost seemed real, and the actors could pretend the ghost was with them on stage.

CORPSE LIGHTS Flickering flames that are seen at times in graveyards. They are caused by gases seeping through the earth from corpses buried in shallow graves.

CROSSROADS GHOST Crossroads were a favourite place to hang criminals whose ghosts remain.

FOLKLORE The fairy tales, legends, beliefs and superstitions in which people over the ages have believed. Many are still believed in today.

GALLOWS GHOST This name is given to the ghost of a person who had been hanged for a crime. The ghost is said to hover near the place of death.

GRAVEYARD GUARDIAN The ghost of the first corpse to be buried in a cemetery. It protected the bodies buried in the graveyard from damage and evil spirits.

HALLUCINATION An image which seems real, even though it does not physically exist.

HAUNTING A situation in which a particular place is visited over and over again by the same ghost. Hauntings may happen anywhere from castles and houses, to shops, ships, motorways and airports. The cause of a haunting is usually some kind of tragic event, often a death, that occurred at the place where the ghost appears. The ghost is a kind of 'visible memory' of the event.

MARSHLIGHTS Shimmering, moving flames that are sometimes seen at night in marshes and other wet areas. They are also known as Will-o'-the wisps. Marshlights are caused when the gases of rotting vegetation begin to burn of their own accord. It was once said that they were the tiny ghosts of young children.

Noises of ghosts

Traditionally, ghosts are not supposed to speak. But folklore is rarely consistent and some legends claimed that ghosts made feeble squeaking sounds like the chirping of birds. The Romans and Greeks believed that ghosts made strange gibbering and muttering sounds.

MEDIUM A person said to have psychic powers than enable him or her to contact the spirits of the dead and to receive their messages. A medium is often consulted by friends and relatives of the dead.

OPTICAL ILLUSION An instance in which people's eyes play tricks on them. What they see at that moment is not really there at all. An example of an optical illusion is the case of a ghostly car that was reported travelling the wrong way down a section of motorway. People imagined they saw the head-lights of another car coming towards them. In fact, a combination of motorway lights, car headlamps and mist had created an optical illusion.

PHANTOM Another term for a ghost. Yet another word for a ghost is spectre.

POLTERGEIST Thought to be a psychic disturbance, during which objects are launched through the air and a tremendous amount of noise is made. One explanation is that poltergeist activity is the result of psychokinesis. The word is German, meaning a noisy spirit.

PSYCHIC The word used to describe forces which have no physical explanation. It includes ESP, ghosts and other supernatural events.

PSYCHIC RESEARCH Investigations that are made by specially trained people trying to find the reasons behind reported ghost hauntings. Investigators sift through the evidence sorting the natural causes from the supernatural ones. The aim of all psychic research is to discover what the forces are which produce ghostly events.

PSYCHOKINESIS The ability to harness psychic forces and direct them at objects to make them move without touching them. Psychokinesis, or PK, is a completely unknown kind of force. Few of the people who have experienced it can control it at will.

SHADES OF THE DEAD A term to describe the dark, shadowy forms in which the spirits of the dead sometimes appear.

SHROUD The white flowing robe that a ghost is said to wear. In fact, shrouds were the sheets in which corpses were wrapped for burial. The ghosts that are most likely to wear them, therefore, are graveyard spirits. Most other ghosts however appear in normal, everyday clothes.

SOUL The spirit of a person. It is not part of the physical body and it cannot be touched or seen. It is believed to be immortal, surviving after the body dies. It used to be thought that a soul that could not pass into the afterlife remained to haunt the Earth as a ghost. One theory imagined that the shape of a soul in the afterlife was that of a butterfly emerging from its chrysalis.

Speaking to a ghost

In the 18th century it was said that a ghost could be commanded to speak if it were addressed firmly. It could be ordered to identify itself and declare its business among living people.

SPIRITUALISM A religious cult which believes among other things that the living can communicate with the spirits of the dead. This is done with a properly conducted ritual called a seance. The seance is led by a medium through whom the spirits can contact the living. Spiritualism began in America in 1848.

SUPERNATURAL Those events, and the forces that create them, which seem to defy the laws of nature and which are, at present, impossible for science to explain. Ghosts and spirits certainly fall into the realm of the supernatural as do telepathy, PK and other psychic forces.

SUPERSTITION A not always rational belief that certain objects and actions have supernatural meanings and in some way can bring about unlikely events, or good or bad luck. One example of a superstitious belief is that if a coin is placed on a

tombstone and is danced around seven times, the ghost within can be enticed into revealing itself, reaching out to snatch the money.

TELEPATHY The mysterious ability to communicate thoughts from one person to another over any distance without using physical means.

Index

Going further

Here are some hints to help you investigate the strange world of ghosts and ghostlore.

The chances of encountering a supernatural presence are rather slim; even psychic researchers rarely claim to see ghosts. A good idea is to interview people who say they have seen a ghost. You can probably find someone in your family if you are lucky, which will make a good start. Write down and collect their stories. You could try drawing a variety of ghosts, using eye witness accounts to base them on.

If you want to look around or photograph a place which is thought to be haunted, remember to ask the owner's permission first. Most people are glad to help if asked but do not like strangers on their land.

Make a study of hauntings in the area where you live. Try making a map like the one shown on pages 18-19. If you can include drawings and photographs on it, so much the better. Make the map poster-sized so you can add more details as you get more information.

Your local library should have lots of books about the world of ghostlore. This list is just a small selection from the many available.

The 1st Armada Book of True Ghost Stories Christine Bernard (Armada)
Ghosts Jane Bord (David and Charles)
Ghosts and Hauntings Aidan Chambers (Longman Young)
Great Ghosts of the World Aidan Chambers (Piccolo)
Ghostly Experiences and **Ghostly Encounters** Susan Dickinson (Lion)
Ghosts, Ghosts, Ghosts Ruth Fenner (Chatto and Windus)
Ghosts and Spirits of Many Lands Edited by Littledale Freya (Target)
Ghosts – the Illustrated History Peter Haining (Sidgwick and Jackson)
Haunted Houses, Ghosts and Spectres Eric Maple and Lynn Myring (Usborne)
The World of Ghosts Alan C Jenkins (Chatto and Windus)
The Haunting and the Haunters Kathleen Lines (Bodley Head)
The Realm of Ghosts Eric Maple (Pan)
Ghosts, Spooks and Spectres Charles Molin (Puffin)

When I was young

The Thirties

NEIL THOMPSON
MEETS
GLYN DAVIES

W
FRANKLIN WATTS
Schools Library and Information Services

Glyn Davies was born in 1924 in the Rhondda Valley in South Wales. He lived with his family in the town of Tonypandy and went to school nearby. After leaving school at the age of fourteen, he worked for a year in a local bakery before becoming a miner in the local colliery. He continued to work as a miner during the Second World War and enrolled as a volunteer fire-fighter to help in case of bombing attacks.

Glyn married a girl from the next village and he and his wife, Sally, continued to live in the Rhondda Valley. In 1980 Glyn was made redundant from his job with the National Coal Board. He became very active in his village community group. He was interviewed for this book aged 65.

This edition 2005

First published in 1991
by Franklin Watts
96 Leonard Street
London
EC2A 4XD

Franklin Watts Australia
Level 17/207 Kent Street
Sydney NSW 2000

© 1991 Franklin Watts

ISBN 0 7496 6329 4

A CIP catalogue record for
this book is available from
the British Library.

Printed in Belgium

Dewey number: 941.083

CONTENTS

Me and my family

I was born in 1924 in the upstairs bedroom of my parents' house in Tonypandy, South Wales. I was christened Glyndwr Davies but I've always been called Glyn. I had two older sisters, Gwladys and Gwyneth, and an older brother, Thomas. Later on my brother Dilwyn was born. He was seven years younger than me.

My father worked in the Gorki colliery. In those days they used horses to pull the coal trucks along underground. Father was a master haulier, which meant that he was in charge of the men working with the horses underground. His job was to keep the miners supplied with empty trucks ready to be filled with coal.

We lived in a rented house in Charles Street. Ours was the end house at the bottom of the hill. Father always said it was holding up the rest of the street.

Me and Dilwyn in our Sunday best.

My father with my brother Dilwyn in my pedal car. I was lucky to be given it. Mine was the first in the village.

In the early 1930s the collieries were privately owned. Branch lines linked them to the main railway network.

My cousins in Welsh national dress.

Our house was like nearly all the other miners' houses in the Rhondda Valley. We had a front room and a kitchen downstairs and three bedrooms upstairs. There was no bathroom, only a cold water tap in the house and an outdoor toilet. We had gas lighting downstairs and in the front bedroom. If you slept in the other rooms you had to take a candle upstairs with you.

Mother cooked on the open fire in the kitchen. We had a coal-burning grate with the oven next to it. It was polished with black lead to make it gleam.

There was no carpet in the house. We had either coconut matting or rag-rugs made from strips of old clothes sewn onto a potato sack. Mother would buy a pennyworth of sand and scour the flagstones in the kitchen. She also cleaned the front doorstep and a stretch of the pavement outside.

The children from our street at the end of the 1920s. My two sisters are to the left of the middle row. The photo was taken from outside our house.

My childhood home now. I live in a house just up the street.

5

My sister Gwyneth was a great polisher. She kept the wooden floor in the front room, which we called the parlour, really shiny. Once when the doctor came to visit my mother, he slipped and fell over on the shiny floor! Mother was resting by the fire in the parlour at the time. The fire was only lit in there at Christmas, or if someone was unwell.

Me and my brothers helped around the house with a few jobs. Father would order a ton of coal to be tipped outside and I'd have to help cart it up the four steps into the coal shed. The one thing we weren't short of was coal.

We had a small garden which Father and I looked after. One year we planted potatoes, cabbages and swedes and the next day went off for an outing. It was dark by the time we got home. Next morning we saw some sheep had escaped into the garden and eaten the lot! We only got a few potatoes out of it. After that we just kept it tidy. The sheep put a damper on us doing any more gardening.

Coal burning stoves were used for cooking and heating water in the 1930s.

The sheep were in the street all the time when I was young. There were more sheep than dogs.

Mother bought the groceries from the Co-op. If you didn't have enough money one week you could still buy things on credit and then settle up at the end of the quarter.

In the 1930s women mostly worked in the home or in domestic service.

Mother did all the cooking and the meals were the same each week. Monday we ate cooked meat from Sunday; Tuesday was fish and home-made chips; Wednesday was lamb chops; Thursday was cold meat and salad. (I was always made to eat the salad. I've been off it ever since.) Friday was home-made faggots and mushy peas bought from a woman down the road; Saturday was bacon and egg. Finally, on Sundays we ate beef, potatoes, peas and cabbage, followed by spotted dick or jam roly-poly.

Some Sundays, for a treat, we had rice pudding or Mother opened a tin of fruit and we had that with condensed milk. In wintertime we had broth or pea soup on a Thursday instead of cold meat.

Hardly anything came in a packet. Most people made their own cakes and jams. A tin of biscuits was kept in the kitchen but we couldn't just help ourselves. We used to sneak in but if Mother caught us we'd get a clip around the ear.

Down the pit

Like nine out of ten men in our valley, my father worked in a colliery. It was difficult to find other work. Once you were fourteen, you left school on a Friday and went down the pit on the Monday. Or if you were clever enough you could train to become a teacher or a preacher.

The pit where my father worked was very near our house. He came home at the end of a shift covered from head to foot with black dust. Mother always had the hot water ready for his bath and then cooked his tea. If his clothes were wet from the pit they had to be hung in front of the fire.

There was never much room at home. But we were better off than a lot of families who had lodgers to help pay the rent. The men often had to share beds. There'd be the day shift and the night shift at the pit and they'd swap over beds between shifts. You were considered a bit posh if your family had the whole house to themselves.

The work underground was always dirty and dangerous. Safety helmets and dust masks were rare in the 1930s.

You should see me on Sunday!

JOHN KNIGHT'S
FAMILY HEALTH SOAP
JOHN KNIGHT

There were few collieries with pit-head baths in the 1930s. Miners had to wait until they got home to wash.

School

When I was four I went to the local school in Llwynypia, a few minutes walk down the hill. It was a mixed school but boys and girls had separate classrooms. From four-to-seven years old we had women teachers. After that the boys had men teachers and the women taught the girls. We had lots of respect for the teachers. We always called them "Sir" or "Miss" if we saw them out on the street in the evenings.

The teachers were pretty strict and I was caned quite a lot. If I was caught talking in class the teacher would say "hand out" and I'd get the cane just on the tip of my fingers. Then when I got home Mother would give me a clip on the ear as well for being naughty at school.

There were between thirty and forty boys in my class but often a lot were away because of illness. Influenza, chickenpox, smallpox and measles were quite common then.

Llwynypia School now. The buildings have changed very little since the 1930s.

The log book from Glyn's school.

The twin sisters (shown at centre) of my wife-to-be, Sally, received prizes for good attendance.

Most days the timetable was the same. In the morning we started at nine o'clock with arithmetic and moved on to history and geography. We went home for dinner at twelve and then came back at half-past one. In the afternoons we did dictation, reading and composition. We had two break-times a day in the yard – a quarter-of-an-hour in the morning, and the same in the afternoon.

We had half-an-hour a week in Welsh. I was hopeless at that and always got nought out of ten. My father understood Welsh but didn't speak it much. My mother didn't understand it at all.

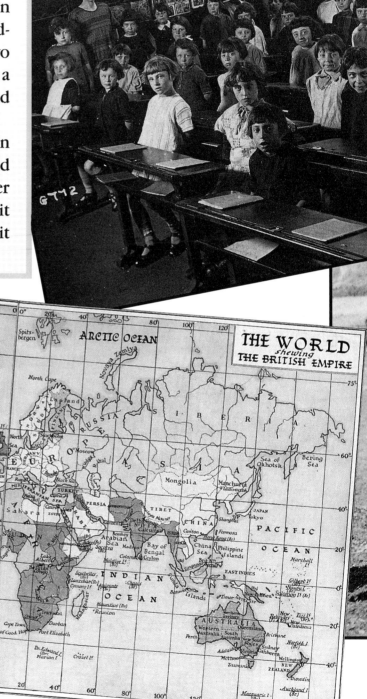

In the 1930s many primary schools were overcrowded. Up to forty children might be in one class.

We learnt all about the British Empire, which was shown by the pink bits on the map.

Llwynypia School Scholarships 1940

R.Samuel, K.Arthur, V.Morgan, G.Brooks, D.Nash, G.Bone, J.Dallimore, M.Thomas, H.Griffiths.
D.Morgan, J.Thomas, Mr. R.Bowen, N.Evans, M.Jones.

Children leaving Llwynypia School with scholarships.

We wore special clothes for school. When we came home we changed into any old patched things just to save the school clothes. All our clothes were handed on from one child to the next.

I was never brilliant at school. There were exams at the end of each summer term and if you didn't pass you had to stay down a year. Somehow I just managed to scrape through each time.

We had one lesson a week in woodwork, and had to walk to a nearby school for it. I made a stool once which I thought was perfect. I took it home and felt quite proud. My father came back from work, had his bath in front of the fire and then sat down on the stool. All the legs broke off and he collapsed on the floor. He called me everything under the sun. He was so cross!

The brightest children won scholarships to go on to secondary school. Otherwise, few parents could afford to keep more than one child at school after they were fourteen. Once you started work you had to give your parents some of your wages each week.

Sundays

Sunday was a special day, it was the only time the collieries were closed. We put on our best suits, or rather our only suits, and went to chapel.

I went to Sunday school in the Bethania Chapel in Tonypandy. The service was in Welsh and, since I couldn't speak it very well, I didn't concentrate much. I had to go though. All the children were regulars at one chapel or another.

There were dozens of chapels and churches in the Rhondda. You could have fitted all the people who lived in the valley into chapels all at once and still have seats left over.

Mother was a staunch follower of chapel. She kept a bible in the parlour on a little table along with a flower vase. She sang in the choir and went along to sisterhood meetings every Tuesday and Thursday night, as well as to all the services on Sunday.

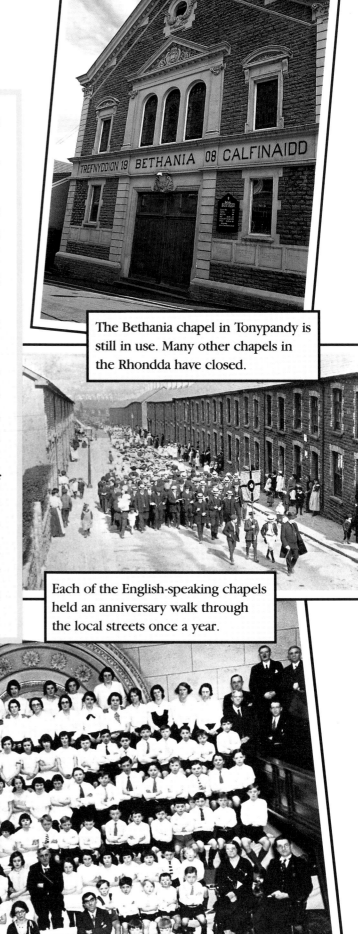

The Bethania chapel in Tonypandy is still in use. Many other chapels in the Rhondda have closed.

Each of the English-speaking chapels held an anniversary walk through the local streets once a year.

Welsh-speaking chapels held festivals of religious songs every year. The choirs were an important part of social life in the Valley communities.

Every year the Sunday school ran an outing to the seaside at Porthcawl or Barry. The preacher always gave each child a newly-minted threepenny bit to spend during the day.

As soon as we arrived we'd all have a cup of tea and a sandwich. Then we'd go down to the beach and put all the beach chairs in a big circle. We had to play inside the circle so we wouldn't get lost.

We were allowed to paddle in the sea but only up to our ankles. Our mothers were frightened that we might drown if we went swimming in the sea. I never learnt to swim, though some of my friends did.

We never went in the cafe unless it started raining. We just took flasks of tea and sandwiches for everyone. We always ended up in the funfair. Mother gave me money for the rides, 2d or 3d they were. After dinner we sang songs and hymns and then went to catch the bus home.

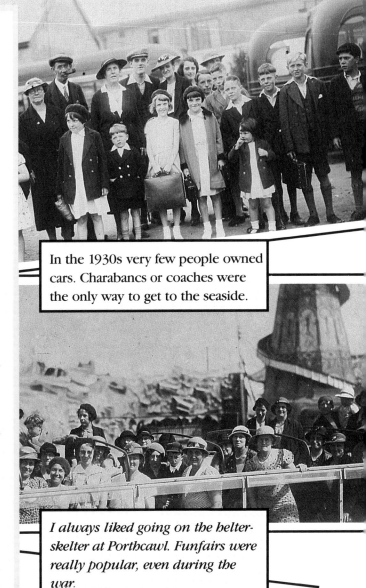

In the 1930s very few people owned cars. Charabancs or coaches were the only way to get to the seaside.

I always liked going on the helter-skelter at Porthcawl. Funfairs were really popular, even during the war.

Porthcawl in the 1930s.

Games and entertainment

We played lots of different games outside in the lane that ran between the rows of houses. We were safe there from the grown-ups. If we played out the front we had to be careful. Hopscotch in the street was a favourite but if you chalked outside someone's house, the chances were they'd come and chase you away. That included my mother. Everyone was so keen on keeping the streets clean in those days.

Sometimes if a grown-up had been bothering us during a game we'd get our own back. We'd go to his house when he was asleep after the night shift. For devilment reasons we'd stuff paper up the mouth of the drainpipe and light it. The hot air going up made a sound like a ship's hooter and would wake up the fellow upstairs. We didn't hang about for long after that!

There was never much spare money in our street. I did a newspaper round when I was ten. I used the money to buy comics. The Dandy *or* The Beano *were the best.*

I collected cigarette cards; ships and planes were my favourites. We swapped them at school so as to get a complete set. We played a game flicking them against the wall — you could win extra ones that way.

Boys in the Rhondda in the 1930s.

Monopoly was first designed in the 1930s and came from America originally.

We made up lots of games with things that we found lying around. We used to make a skipping rope from the cord that came tied round boxes of oranges. Three of those tied together would stretch from one side of the road to the other.

We played hook and wheel. If we were lucky the colliery blacksmith would make us a wheel. We had a metal hook to go with it to make it spin along the road. We got ball bearings from the colliery and played with them. We dug three or four holes in the lane behind the houses and played something like marbles.

We had to be in by five o'clock in the winter and by half-eight in the summer. If our parents had to shout for us a second time we'd get a clip around the ear.

Children playing with hook and wheel in Clydach Vale earlier in the 20th century. The game was still popular in the 1930s.

When we were playing football in the street we'd keep a look out for the policeman's helmet. Where we lived the policemen were all six-footers. If we saw one we'd all scatter. We'd never stand up to a policeman. If we broke a window we had to pay for it out of our pocket money, so we made sure that didn't happen too often.

On Sunday afternoons Charles Street fielded a football team that went up the mountain to play. We weren't really meant to go and play on a Sunday so if anyone saw us we were told off.

I supported Cardiff City – they were a pretty good soccer team. We went down on special trains to Cardiff for the matches. We only ever had enough money for the train and the entrance to the match. There was no fun and games afterwards. We just came straight home again.

Although rugby was the traditional sport of South Wales, English immigrants into Wales brought the game of soccer with them, and it became increasingly popular.

Going to the cinema

I often went to the pictures in Tonypandy. There were two cinemas then, the Picturedrome and the Empire. Before the film started we went to the greengrocers and bought a halfpenny swede. Mother would peel it for us to eat in the cinema.

We sat in the "gods" upstairs on hard wooden planks with no backs to them. Then we used to hide in the toilets so we could see the film a second time around without paying! We were lucky then if we could afford to go each week but we didn't like missing an episode of the Saturday morning serial. The children's serial was so popular everyone called it the "penny rush". I liked the *Buck Rogers* serial – it would be on each week for months.

Flash Gordon was another children's film serial at this time.

There was a new *Tarzan* film almost every year throughout the 1930s and 1940s.

Film-going was so popular that queues used to form all down the street.

17

Radio days

We listened to the radio a lot at home. For a while we had piped radio from radio rentals. There were four wires running along the street and into each house down the outside wall. Indoors we had a box with a speaker and just one knob on it for the volume. Inside was a dry battery and an accumulator which had to be charged once a week.

There was one switch with three positions, middle was off, up was the Home Service and down the Light Programme. That was the choice then. We called it "home and away".

We liked listening to Big Band music; Henry Hall, Billy Cotton and *Saturday Night Music Hall*. We liked the comedians as well; Bennie Lyon, Gladys Morgan and a show called *Welsh Rarebit*.

The BBC was the only broadcasting station in the 1930s. The Home Service provided news and drama. The Light Programme covered popular music.

I really liked listening to Billy Cotton and his band on the radio.

The Coronation

The King's coronation in May 1937 was a great event for us. We were given a holiday from school since there were celebrations in all the streets. Just before the big day, the school gave out coronation mugs for the boys and coronation cups and saucers for the girls.

There were tables out in all the streets. Flowers and colourful flags decorated the streets. After we'd eaten the celebration meal there was dancing outside, to music from a wind-up gramophone. The party went on until it was dark. We only had a few gas lamps in the street so we went indoors quite early.

In 1937 George VI was crowned. The previous year his brother, Edward VIII abdicated in order to marry the divorcee, Wallis Simpson.

We had a big party just up the hill from us on Coronation Day.

TIT-BITS
CORONATION SOUVENIR

THEIR MAJESTIES KING GEORGE VI AND QUEEN ELIZABETH

SUPPLEMENT TO "TIT-BITS"

MAY 15, 1937

CORONATION 1937

T. M. KING GEORGE VI.
AND QUEEN ELIZABETH

Build up to war

At home we listened to the wireless and heard the news of Hitler invading other countries. I remember hearing the British prime minister, Neville Chamberlain, saying, "I believe it is peace for our time", after he had met with Hitler in Munich. Lots of young men, including my older brother, went off to join up in the forces.

At school, we didn't take much notice until just before war was declared. The teachers told us to be prepared for air raid warnings and we had to practise air raid drill. The cellar of the school was turned into bomb shelters. We practised running in there with our gas masks.

I couldn't go into the forces myself, since by the time I reached the right age I was already working in the pit. The country needed coal to keep going during the war so I was needed there. I did join up as a volunteer firefighter later on but Tonypandy never was bombed. However, my sister, Gwladys, put out an incendiary bomb which hit the hospital where she was working in Cardiff.

Children throughout Britain were issued with gas masks. They were never actually needed.

Neville Chamberlain returning from Munich after meeting with Hitler.

Bomb shelters were quickly set up in the 1930s once war seemed definite.

Holidays

We never went away on holiday as a family. There wasn't enough money to stretch to that. The miners only got two weeks holiday a year, which was called "miners' fortnight". Even the pit-ponies had a break then. It was the only time all year that they saw life above ground.

In the August school holidays some of us boys used to go camping up on the mountain. We had to make our own tents. First we went to the Co-op and bought some of the big sacks that sugar came in. Then we cut them open and sewed them together to make simple tents. There'd be four or five of us boys in each one.

At Christmas there was always a funfair in Tonypandy. On New Year's Eve it would be absolutely packed. For half-an-hour after midnight, when the church bells and the factory hooter sounded, all the rides were free.

Mother made our Christmas pudding, of course. Christmas was also the only time in the year when we ate fresh fruit.

Pit ponies loading onto a train on the way to their "holiday".

Moving on

When I was twelve my sister Gwladys got married and moved out to Port Talbot. Her husband had a job in the steel works down there. Most girls round us went into service after they left school. They worked as maids for one of the colliery managers or went away to get a job in the house of a rich family. Gwladys and my other sister ended up nursing.

My older brother worked in the Gorki colliery for a bit. Then he signed up with the Royal Air Force just before the war.

My sister, Gwladys, at the time she left home.

After the First World War ended, the demand for coal was reduced. Many collieries were closed for some of the week.

My brother in his RAF uniform. He was one of the ground crew.

The depression

We were lucky that Father had work all through the 1930s. There was a lot of unemployment in the pits and nowhere much else to get a job. Most of the South Wales miners were on short-time working and families had very little to live on.

There were bad times when many people couldn't even afford breakfast. They'd go to the Salvation Army hall where there was sometimes free food. You could have bread, margarine and cocoa; or bread, jam and cocoa. You couldn't have margarine and jam at the same time.

Miners who were out of work couldn't get coal. They had to pick it off the mountain. This was illegal but the police usually turned a blind eye.

In 1936, unemployed shipyard workers marched 300 miles from Jarrow to London to draw attention to the problem of unemployment.

In the 1930s one in three men in the Rhondda were unemployed. Many families left to look for work elsewhere. Houses were just left empty.

JARROW PETITION

Starting work

When I left school at fourteen I got a job through my uncle. He was the delivery man for the local bakery. I worked on the bread deliveries from seven in the morning until six in the evening, Monday to Thursday. Then on Friday and Saturday I worked until nine-thirty in the evening. For all this I earned seven shillings and sixpence a week. After a few months I started in the bake-house wheeling sacks of flour for fifteen shillings a week.

When I was fifteen my father had an accident in the colliery and broke both his legs. He was off work for some time and we didn't have enough to live on.

My wage from the bakery wasn't much so I went along, cap in hand, to the colliery manager to ask for a job. He said, "Does your father work here?". I said, "Yes, sir". He asked me my father's name and when I told him he said, "Start on Monday".

Miners were issued with a safety lamp before going underground.

FEATHERY FLAKE

the quality Self Raising FLOUR

For delightful puddings

Many deliveries were made by horse-drawn vehicles until the end of the 1930s.

OWENS & SONS Brynleg Bakery YSTRAD

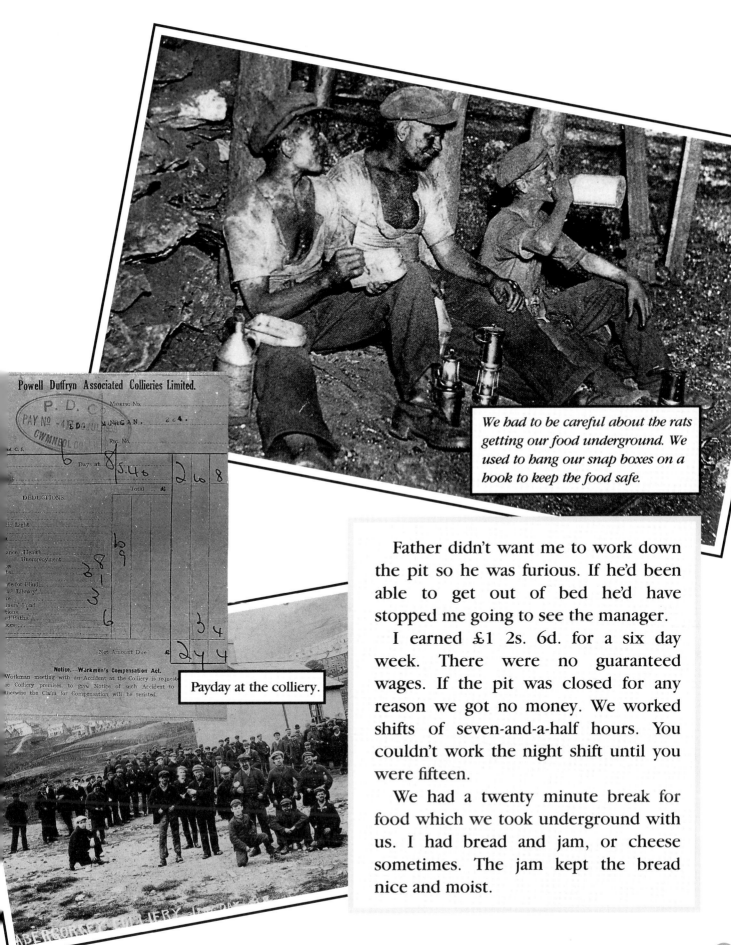

We had to be careful about the rats getting our food underground. We used to hang our snap boxes on a hook to keep the food safe.

Powell Duffryn Associated Collieries Limited.

Payday at the colliery.

Father didn't want me to work down the pit so he was furious. If he'd been able to get out of bed he'd have stopped me going to see the manager.

I earned £1 2s. 6d. for a six day week. There were no guaranteed wages. If the pit was closed for any reason we got no money. We worked shifts of seven-and-a-half hours. You couldn't work the night shift until you were fifteen.

We had a twenty minute break for food which we took underground with us. I had bread and jam, or cheese sometimes. The jam kept the bread nice and moist.

A miner's life

I worked underground for eleven years until I developed dermatitis. My skin was really affected and the doctor said I couldn't work on the coal face any more. I got a job as a surface worker hauling the waste from the colliery around the slag heaps. When the Cambrian closed in 1966 I was put into a mobile team working on the rail tracks. I worked until 1980 when I was made redundant and couldn't find another job. I haven't worked since. I was considered too old at 55 to get another job.

My wife and I live in what was my mother-in-law's house up the hill from where I was born. I'm now deputy chairman of the local community committee. We've raised money to convert the old police station into a social centre. All that organising keeps me pretty busy.

My wife, Sally, and I on our wedding day in 1956.

The site of the Cambrian colliery now. There were fifty pits in the Rhondda Valley in the 1930s. Now there are none.

I was given a model miner's lamp as a retirement present.

In the News

These are some of the important events
which happened during Glyn's childhood.

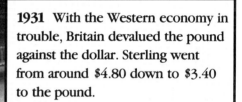

1930 In India, Mahatma Gandhi
began a campaign of civil
disobedience against the British
colonial government.

1931 With the Western economy in
trouble, Britain devalued the pound
against the dollar. Sterling went
from around $4.80 down to $3.40
to the pound.

1932 Franklin Roosevelt was
elected President of The United
States of America.

1933 Adolf Hitler became Chancellor of Germany. The Nazis began a violent campaign against any opposition.

1934 After an explosion in Wrexham pit, 262 miners lost their lives.

1935 Sir Malcolm Campbell set a world record of 301 mph in his car, Bluebird.

1936 Jesse Owens won four gold medals at the Berlin Olympic Games. Hitler refused to even shake his hand.

1937 The German air force bombed Guernica in Spain in support of the fascist government there.

1938 Adolf Hitler took control of Austria. Jews were not allowed to vote in a referendum on Austria's union with Germany.

1939 After Hitler's invasion of Poland, the British government declared war with Germany.

Things to do

Some of your relatives or neighbours will have memories of the 1930s. Their experiences may have been very different from those of Glyn Davies. Show them this book and ask them how their lives in the 1930s compared with his.

If you have a cassette recorder you could tape their memories. Before you visit people, make a list of the things you want to talk about – for example, toys and games, radio, films and sports. Most school leavers in the 1930s started work at fourteen. Find out what sort of jobs were available then. Ask about the different jobs done by men and women in the 1930s.

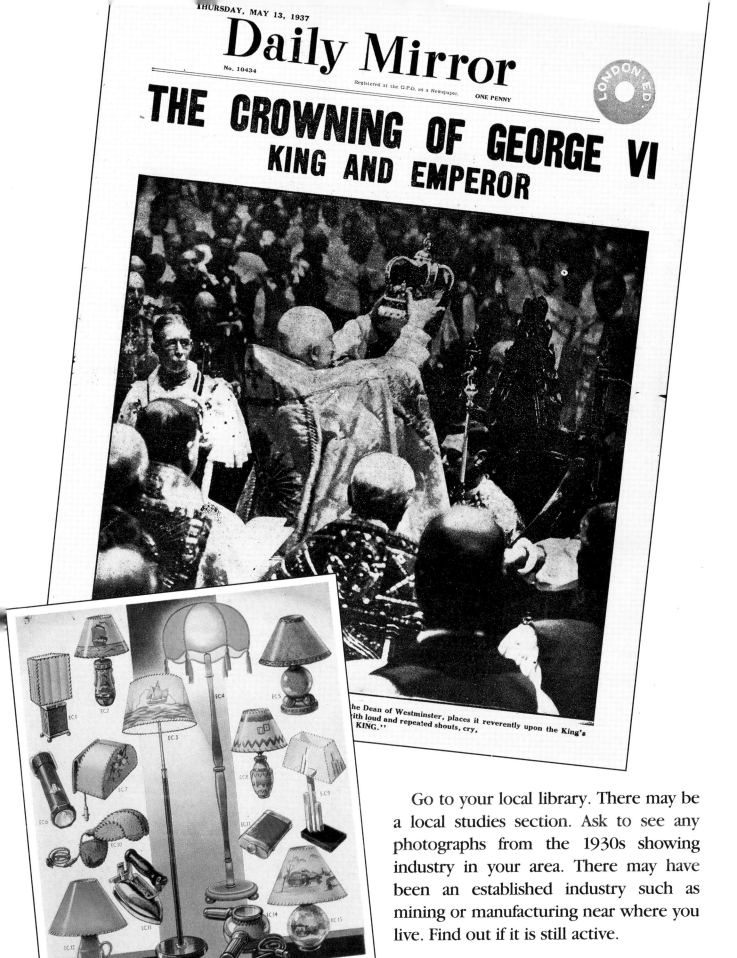

Daily Mirror

No. 10434

Registered at the G.P.O. as a Newspaper.   ONE PENNY

LONDON E.D.

THE CROWNING OF GEORGE VI
KING AND EMPEROR

he Dean of Westminster, places it reverently upon the King's ith loud and repeated shouts, cry, KING."

Go to your local library. There may be a local studies section. Ask to see any photographs from the 1930s showing industry in your area. There may have been an established industry such as mining or manufacturing near where you live. Find out if it is still active.

Index

Series design: David Bennett
Design: Sally Boothroyd
Editor: Sarah Ridley

Acknowledgements: the author
and publisher would like to thank
Glyn and Sally Davies, Selwyn
Jones, Greg Reynolds, Bill Jones,
Dave Maddox, Ron Howells and
William John Thomas for their
help with this book.

Photographs: Cyril Batstone 8t,
10-11t, 15b, 24b, 25t; BFI Stills,
posters and designs 17br; Cynon
Valley Libraries 6br; Mary Evans
Picture Library 31b; Hulton
Picture Company 18b, 27b, 28b;
thanks to Byron Jones 25c; Kobal
front cover (bl), 17bl; thanks to
Llwynypia School 9c, 11t; thanks
to Mid-Glamorgan County Council
Education Authority 18c; National
Museum of Wales front cover (cl),
4bl, 6bl, 8b, 11b, 14b, 20b, 21b,
22b, 23t, 23bl, 24t, 25b; National
Museum of Wales/Spencer Powell
Collection 7tl; Robert Opie 6t, 7tr,
8c, 14t, 15t, 17t, 18t, 19c, 24c,
30br; Popperfoto 21t, 21c, 23br,
28tl, 29t, 29cl, 29b; Porthcawl
Museum 13b, 30cr; thanks to
Richard Shepherd 16; Neil
Thomson frontispiece, 5b, 9t, 12t,
26b; Topham Picture Source 27t,
27c, 28cr, 29cr; Treorchy Library,
Rhondda Borough Council 12c,
12b.

A CIP catalogue record for this
book is available from the British
Library.